5

Time was, Zomo wanted *more* than
cleverness — he wanted wisdom!
He went to Sky God and asked for it.

"Zomo, it is not so simple," said Sky God.
"To get wisdom, you must earn it."

7

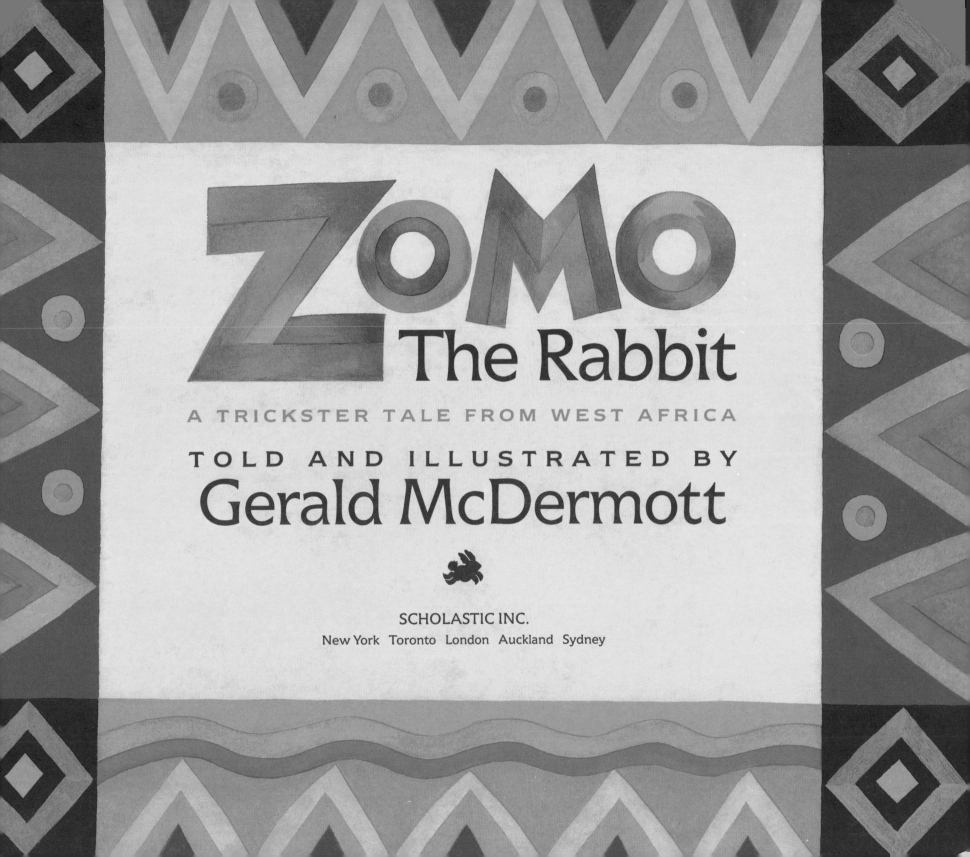

ZOMO
The Rabbit

A TRICKSTER TALE FROM WEST AFRICA

TOLD AND ILLUSTRATED BY
Gerald McDermott

SCHOLASTIC INC.

New York Toronto London Auckland Sydney

Copyright © 1992 by Gerald McDermott.
All rights reserved. Published by Scholastic Inc.,
555 Broadway, New York, NY 10012, by arrangement
with Harcourt Brace & Company.
The paintings in this book were done in gouache
on heavyweight hot-press watercolor paper.
The display type and text type were set in Icone 55
by Thompson Type, San Diego, California.
Typography designed by Lydia D'moch.
Printed in the U.S.A.
ISBN 0-590-48947-X

2 3 4 5 6 7 8 9 10   08   01 00 99 98 97 96

Zomo the Rabbit is a prominent member of the
family of animal tricksters that populate the
traditional tales of West Africa. These humorous
stories of mischief and cunning are told to
instruct as well as to entertain and have been
kept alive by the powerful oral traditions of the
African peoples.

There are many links between these African
tales and their cultural descendants in the New
World. Zomo, though separated from his origins
in Hausaland, Nigeria, by an ocean and several
centuries, lives on as Cunny Rabbit or Compere
Lapin in the Caribbean and as Brer Rabbit in the
United States.

Like tricksters in storytelling traditions around
the world, the fleet-footed Zomo outwits his
larger foes with guile and trickery. And like his
African cousins Spider and Tortoise, he uses his
wit to gain wisdom.

—G. M.

For Jimena

Zomo!

Zomo the rabbit.
He is not big.
He is not strong.
But he is very clever.

"How?" asked Zomo.

"You must do three impossible things," answered Sky God. "First, bring me the scales of Big Fish in the sea. Second, bring me the milk of Wild Cow. Third, bring me the tooth of Leopard."

"I will try," said Zomo.

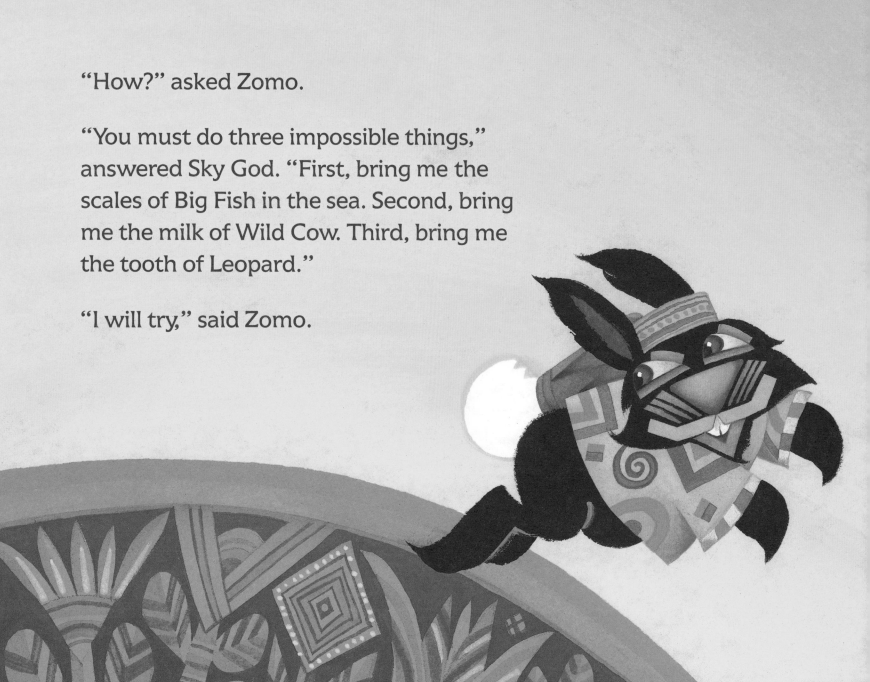

9

Zomo went to the edge of the sea.
He began to play his drum.
He played so loud his drumbeats went
down to the bottom of the sea.

10

Deep below, Big Fish heard the music of the drum.

Big Fish came up out of the water.
He danced on the sand.

Faster and faster, Zomo beat his drum.
Faster and faster, Big Fish danced.

Big Fish danced so fast his scales fell off.

Big Fish was naked.

13

Splash! He jumped back into the sea.

Quickly, Zomo scooped up the fish scales in his hat and hopped into the forest.

In the forest, Zomo climbed a palm tree.
He looked all around.
Then he saw Wild Cow.

"Ha!" laughed Zomo.
"You are not so big!
You are not strong!"

16

"Who is that laughing at me?" asked Wild Cow.

17

"It is me," called Zomo. "I say you are not even strong enough to knock down this little tree."

Wild Cow got angry.
She ran at the tree to knock it down.

Thump! She hit that tree.
But the palm tree was soft.
Her horns got stuck.

Quickly, Zomo slid down
the tree.

He turned his drum upside down and filled it with milk.

By the time Wild Cow got unstuck, Zomo was far away.

21

Zomo took the path to the top of
a high hill.
It was the hill where Leopard
walked every day.
Zomo tipped his hat and sprinkled
a few fish scales on the path.

Zomo tipped his drum and spilled
a few drops of milk on the path.

Then Zomo went to the bottom of the hill.
He hid behind a rock.

23

Soon Leopard came walking over the hill.
He slipped on the slippery scales and
the milk.

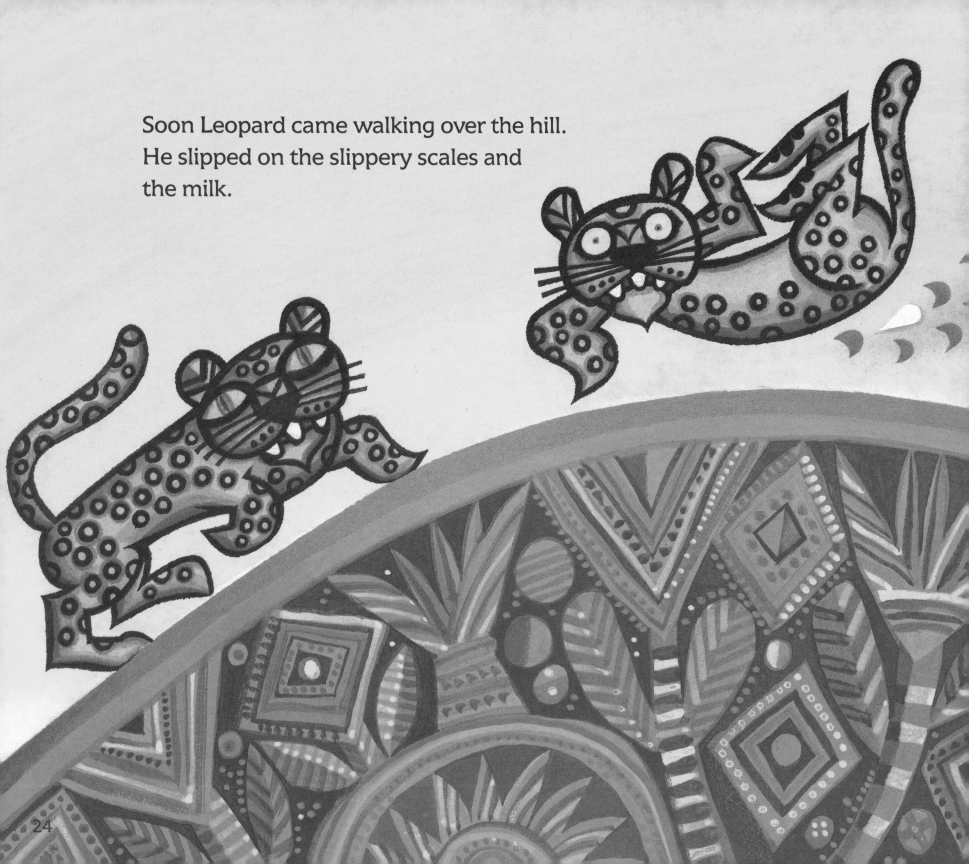

He rolled down the hill.

Bump! Leopard hit the rock.
His tooth popped out.

Up jumped Zomo.
He caught that tooth.
Quickly, he hopped away.

Zomo took the scales of Big Fish,
the milk of Wild Cow,
and the tooth of Leopard to Sky God.

Sky God smiled upon Zomo.
"You are clever enough to do
the impossible," he said.
"Now I will give you wisdom."

Sky God spoke.
Zomo listened.

28

"Three things in this world are worth having:
courage, good sense, and caution," said Sky God.
"Little rabbit, you have lots of courage, a bit of sense,
but no caution. So next time you see Big Fish, or
Wild Cow, or Leopard . . .

. . . better run fast!"

Zomo is not big.
Zomo is not strong.
But now Zomo has wisdom.
And he is very, very fast.